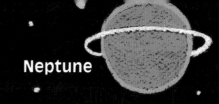

Neptune

Saturn

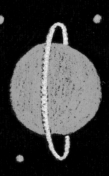

Uranus

Pluto

Dogs in Space

VOYAGER BOOKS
HARCOURT, INC.
ORLANDO AUSTIN NEW YORK SAN DIEGO LONDON

First Voyager Books edition 1996

Voyager Books is a registered trademark of Harcourt, Inc..

Printed in Singapore

Library of Congress Cataloging-in-Publication Data
Coffelt, Nancy.
Dogs in space/by Nancy Coffelt.
p.   cm.
"Voyager Books."
Summary: Dogs in space visit each of the planets in the solar
system, finding no one at home anywhere, and return to Earth.
ISBN 978-0-15-200440-8
ISBN 978-0-15-201004-1 pb
[1. Planets — Fiction.   2. Solar system —Fiction.   3. Dogs — Fiction.]   I. Title.
PZ7.C658Do   1993
[E] — dc20   92-29036

H J L N P O O M K I

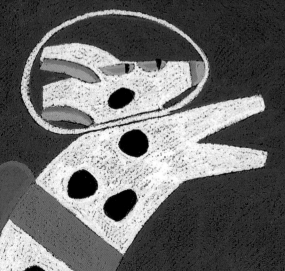

The illustrations in this book were done
in Caran D'ache oil pastels on black Canson paper.
The display and text type were set in Antique Olive
by Thompson Type, San Diego, California.
Color separations by Bright Arts, Ltd., Hong Kong
Printed and bound by Tien Wah Press, Singapore
Production supervision by Warren Wallerstein and Diana Ford
Designed by Camilla Filancia

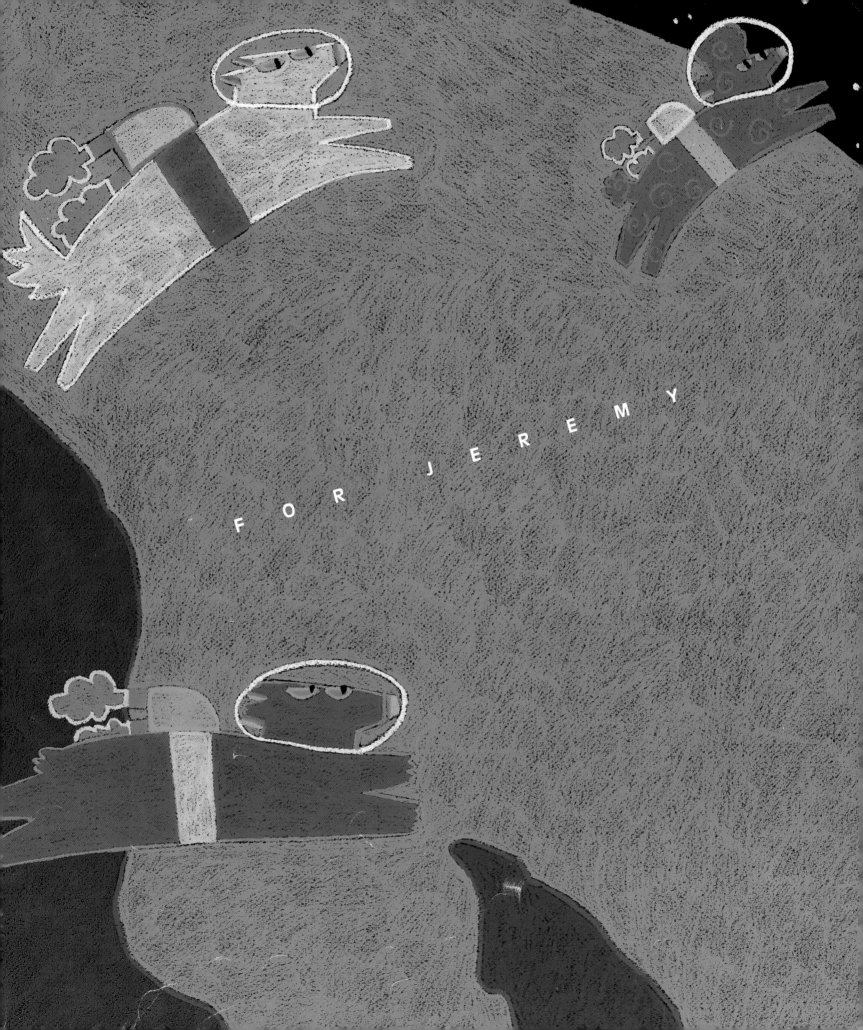

FOR JEREMY

Space dogs blast off from Earth
for the Great Solar System Tour.

Their first stop is Mercury, the planet closest to the Sun.

Ouch! It's too hot on Mercury for dogs in space.
The Sun is so strong that dogs in space need sunglasses.

And there is no one home,
so dogs in space race to Venus.

And there is no one home on Venus, so dogs in space fly to Mars, the "Red Planet."

Look out for that dust storm!

Ah-choo!
Dogs in space sneeze red dust on the planet Mars.

But there is no one home on Mars, either,
so dogs in space head toward giant Jupiter.

Dogs in space have a long way to go.

They have to pass through the Asteroid Belt.

Dogs in space dodge asteroids
on their way to Jupiter.

How big is that red spot, anyway?

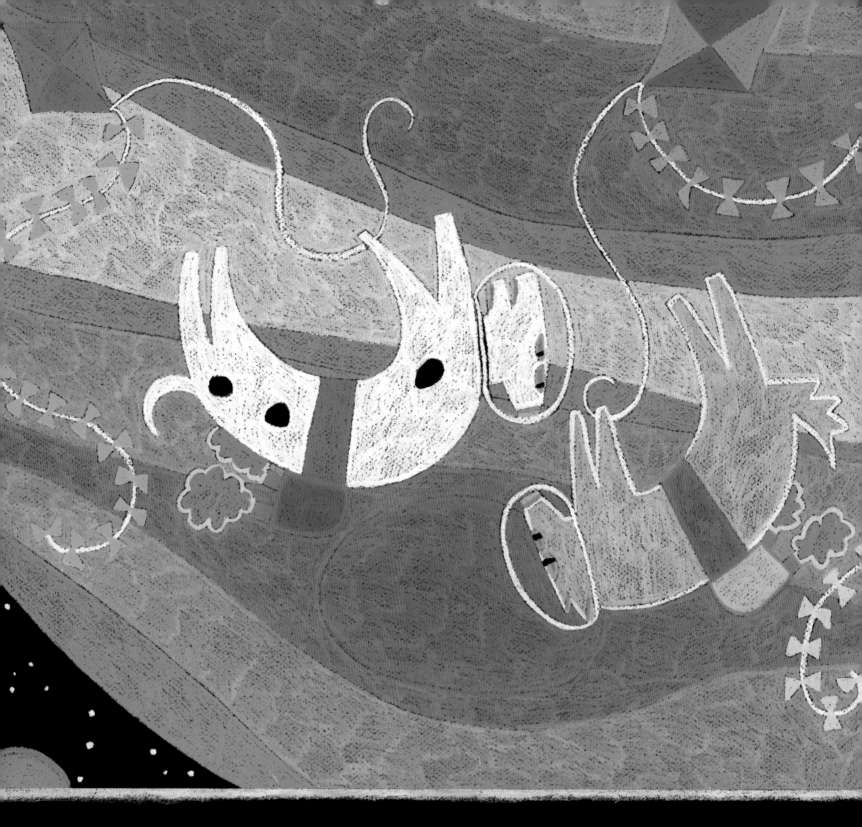

The wind blows hard on the planet Jupiter.
Dogs in space fly kites there. But . . .

there is no one home on Jupiter,
so dogs in space zoom to Saturn.

 Love those rings!

Dogs in space play hide-and-seek among
the eighteen moons of Saturn. But . . .

there is no one to play with on the planet Saturn.

Uranus is the one tipped on its side.

Dogs in space spin sideways on the planet Uranus.

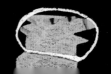

Wheee!

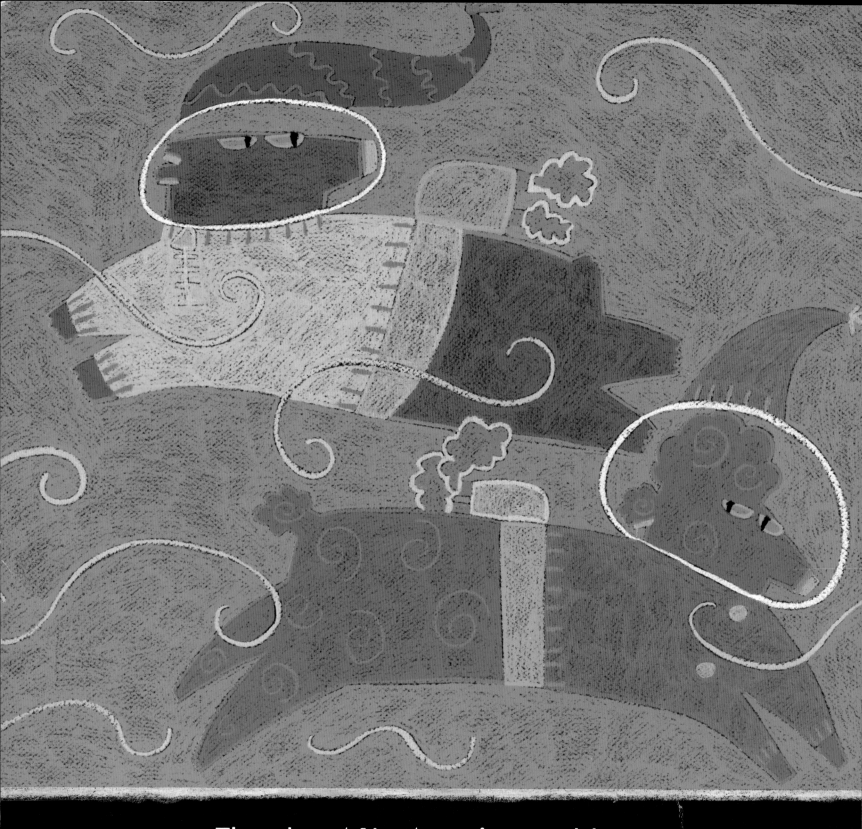

The planet Neptune is so cold,
dogs in space need heavy sweaters.

And there is no one home on Uranus and Neptune,
so dogs in space soar all the way to Pluto, the smallest planet.

Where's the light switch?

There is very little light on Pluto.
Dogs in space are far from the Sun.

They are very near the edge of the Solar System,
where it is cold and dark and lonely.

Even though there are no other dogs in space,
or people, either, dogs in space like space.

There are no cats in space. There are no fleas in space.
Dogs in space can shed hair in zero gravity.

But . . . there are no soft laps in space,
no crunchy dog bones, and no warm fires.

And there is no one to play with, so . . . .

dogs in space go home, for now.

The Great Solar System Tour

GRAVITY

Every object in the universe invisibly pulls on and is pulled toward every other object. We call this invisible pulling, or attraction between objects, *gravity*. The amount of an object's gravity depends on the *mass* of the object. Small objects, such as an apple or a person or even a skyscraper, have very little mass and therefore little gravity. Large objects, such as planets, stars, and galaxies, have much more mass and enormous gravity. Because Earth is so massive, its gravity is very strong and pulls everything on Earth to its surface.

Earth's gravity extends through space to pull on the Moon, too, making it circle, or *orbit*, the Earth about once every twenty-eight days.

The largest object in the Solar System, the Sun, has the strongest gravity. Its gravity is so strong that it is able to reach across billions of kilometers and alter the planets' routes through space. If not for the Sun's pull, the planets would move in straight lines through space. But the Sun's gravity adjusts the planets' paths so that they circle around it.

THE SOLAR SYSTEM

The Solar System is what we call the family of nine planets, their moons, and the countless other celestial bodies that circle the Sun.

Although the nine planets are quite different from one another, there are some basic similarities all of them share:

Each is surrounded by a layer of gases called an *atmosphere*. You breathe in the air of Earth's atmosphere every day.

Each planet spins like a top, turning on an invisible line called its *axis*. On Earth, this spin creates day and night, because the planet rotates once every twenty-four hours, turning different sides to face the sun.

Each planet orbits the Sun. No orbit is perfectly circular — most are slightly oval or elliptical. It takes the Earth just over 365 days, or one year, to complete one orbit.

Most of the planets have moons that orbit them just as the planets orbit the Sun. These moons range in size from a few kilometers across to larger than Pluto, the smallest planet. Saturn has the most known moons in the Solar System, with eighteen, while Earth has only one, and Venus and Mercury none at all. Astronomers speak of a planet's *known* moons when they suspect that there may be more moons than they've spotted so far.

THE SUN

Diameter:
1,400,000 kilometers
(868,000 miles)
Temperature:
14,000,000° Celsius
(25,200,000° Fahrenheit)

Even though we see the stars only as points of light, each one is as large and bright as our local star, the Sun. The Sun is a giant ball of hydrogen gas almost a thousand times more massive than all of the planets put together. It is so massive, in fact, and its gravity so strong, that the enormous pressures at its center fuse hydrogen molecules into helium, creating energy and bathing the Solar System with heat and light.

MERCURY

Diameter:
4,878 kilometers
(3,024 miles)
Average distance from Sun:
57,910,000 kilometers
(35,904,200 miles)
Temperature:
−180° to +430° Celsius
(−292° to +805° F.)
Ranking in terms of size:
Eight
Number of moons:
Zero

Mercury is the second smallest planet in the Solar System and the planet closest to the Sun. Because the Sun is so close, temperatures on the side of Mercury facing the Sun can reach 430° Celsius, but on the side facing away from the Sun it is a freezing −180° C. Mercury is a brown, barren, heavily cratered planet with almost no atmosphere and no moons. It rotates very slowly — its day (sunrise to sunrise) is twice as long as its year (the time it takes to orbit the Sun).

VENUS

Diameter:
12,103 kilometers
(7,504 miles)
Average distance from Sun:
108,200,000 kilometers
(67,084,000 miles)
Temperature:
465° Celsius
(870° F.)
Ranking in terms of size:
Six
Number of moons:
Zero

Although it is a planet and not a star, Venus is called both the "morning star" and the "evening star" because those are the times when it is most easily seen from Earth. Venus is only slightly

smaller than Earth but is vastly different. Because of the thick yellow-brown clouds that cover its surface, heat and radiation cannot easily escape, making it the hottest planet in the Solar System. Venus is even hotter than Mercury, despite the fact that Venus is farther away from the Sun.

EARTH

Diameter:
12,756 kilometers
(7,909 miles)
Average distance from Sun:
149,600,000 kilometers
(92,752,000 miles)
Temperature:
−70° to +55° Celsius
(−94° to +131° F.)
Ranking in terms of size:
Five
Number of moons:
One

Earth is the middle planet in size: four planets are smaller and four are larger. It is the only planet in the Solar System with liquid water and, as a result, the only planet with life. Two-thirds of Earth's surface is covered with water. The rest of the planet's surface ranges from dry deserts to lush tropical forests to frozen tundra. The combination of Earth's temperature, atmosphere, and large oceans creates an environment that can support the plants, animals, and people that live on the planet. Earth's one moon, covered with craters and dark plains of dust, is one-fourth the size of Earth and has no atmosphere.

MARS

Diameter:
6,786 kilometers
(4,207 miles)
Average distance from Sun:
227,940,000 kilometers
(141,322,800 miles)
Temperature:
−120° to −25° Celsius
(−184° to −13° F.)
Ranking in terms of size:
Seven
Number of moons:
Two

Mars is the third smallest planet in the Solar System and is sometimes called the "Red Planet" because of its rusty color. Though it is much smaller than Earth, Mars is similar in a number of ways — it has mountains, deserts, canyons, and volcanoes. In addition, the surface of Mars changes visibly with the seasons: its white polar ice caps grow and shrink, and huge yearly dust storms engulf areas of the planet. Mars is dusty, rocky, and has a thin atmosphere of carbon dioxide gas. Mars's two small moons are called Phobos and Deimos.

Astronomers once thought that Mars might be a probable home for extraterrestrial life because of what appeared to be canals and patches of vegetation that changed with the seasons. They later learned that what they thought were canals were merely optical illusions. And the "patches of vegetation" were actually areas of darker rock that were covered and uncovered by dust storms.

THE ASTEROIDS

The Main Asteroid Belts lie between the orbits of Mars and Jupiter and are composed of thousands and thousands of chunks of rock that range in size from a few thousand meters to hundreds of kilometers across. But although the asteroids extend over a vast area of space, if all of them were put together they still would not be as large as our Moon. No one knows for sure why the asteroids never joined together to form a planet; one theory suggests that Jupiter's massive gravity makes a tenth planet in the space between Mars and Jupiter impossible.

JUPITER

Diameter:
142,984 kilometers
(88,650 miles)
Average distance from Sun:
778,330,000 kilometers
(482,564,600 miles)
Atmospheric temperature:
−150° Celsius
(−238° F.)
Ranking in terms of size:
One
Number of known moons:
Sixteen

Jupiter is by far the largest planet in the Solar System — larger than all the other planets put together. It is the first of the four "gas giants" (Jupiter, Saturn, Uranus, and Neptune), meaning that it is made mostly of light gases such as hydrogen and helium. Its atmosphere is striped with bands of orange, reddish brown, and yellow clouds.

Jupiter rotates rapidly, which creates fierce winds and huge storms and causes the planet to bulge outward so that it is slightly oval in shape, wider than it is tall. The biggest of the storms is called the Great Red Spot, which is more than three times as wide as the Earth. In addition to its two very faint rings, Jupiter has sixteen moons, four of which (Ganymede, Callisto, Io, and Europa) are larger than Pluto. One of these, Io, is covered with active volcanoes.

SATURN

Diameter:
120,536 kilometers
(74,732 miles)
Average distance from Sun:
1,426,980,000 kilometers
(884,727,600 miles)
Atmospheric temperature:
−180° Celsius
(−292° F.)
Ranking in terms of size:
Two
Number of known moons:
Eighteen

Saturn is the second largest planet in the Solar System and, despite its dull ocher color, is the most easily recognized because of its beautiful ring system. The second of the gas giants, Saturn is made mostly of hydrogen and helium, much like its neighbor Jupiter. But whereas Jupiter's two rings are faint and unimpressive, Saturn's rings — each composed of thousands of smaller rings — are striking and bright and easy to see from Earth with a small telescope. The rings are made of billions of particles of dust and ice that vary in size from a few centimeters to more than ten meters across. Titan, one of Saturn's eighteen moons, is the only moon in the Solar System to have a planetlike atmosphere.

URANUS

Diameter:
51,118 kilometers
(31,693 miles)
Average distance from Sun:
2,870,990,000 kilometers
(1,780,013,800 miles)
Atmospheric temperature:
−210° Celsius
(−346° F.)
Ranking in terms of size:
Three
Number of known moons:
Fifteen

The third largest planet in the Solar System and the third gas giant, Uranus is the only planet to spin on its side. Astronomers are baffled as to why. Uranus's light blue atmosphere is made mostly of hydrogen and helium. In addition to its fifteen moons, Uranus is encircled by at least eleven narrow rings, which are composed of large, dark rocks. The rings and the moons circle the planet in the same direction as it rotates.

NEPTUNE

Diameter:
49,528 kilometers
(30,707 miles)
Average distance from Sun:
4,497,070,000 kilometers
(2,788,183,400 miles)
Atmospheric temperature:
−210° Celsius
(−346° F.)
Ranking in terms of size:
Four
Number of known moons:
Eight

Bright blue Neptune is the fourth largest planet in the Solar System and the smallest of the gas giants. It is home to the fastest winds in the Solar System, which blow around the planet in a direction opposite to its spin. Neptune has four rings — two broad ones and two narrow ones — as well as eight known moons. Two of the smaller moons, Galatea and Despoina, have been nicknamed "shepherd moons." They orbit in the spaces between the two narrow rings — keeping the ring particles in a solid, dark line and the space between the rings clear. Because Pluto has an exaggerated orbit, Neptune becomes the farthest planet from the Sun for 20 out of every 250 years.

PLUTO

Diameter:
2,284 kilometers
(1,417 miles)
Average distance from Sun:
5,913,520,000 kilometers
(3,666,382,400 miles)
Temperature:
−220° Celsius
(−364° F.)
Ranking in terms of size:
Nine
Number of known moons:
One

Pluto, discovered in 1930, is the smallest planet and, for 230 years of its almost 250-year orbit, it is the outermost planet in the Solar System. Because it is so far from the Sun, it also has the coldest surface temperature of all the planets — a chilly −220° Celsius. Its atmosphere of methane gas is usually frozen in the form of a methane frost — except at Pluto's closest approach to the Sun. The planet is pinkish brown, and its one moon, Charon, is more than half as big as Pluto.

PLANET 10?

Diameter: ?
Average distance from Sun: ?
Temperature: ?
Ranking in terms of size: ?
Number of known moons: ?

Because of irregularities in the orbits of Uranus and Neptune, many astronomers suspect that out beyond the orbit of Pluto there may be another planet whose gravity is affecting the outer planets. But, as yet, no one has been able to locate it.

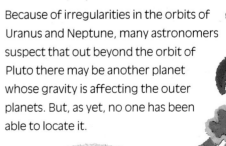

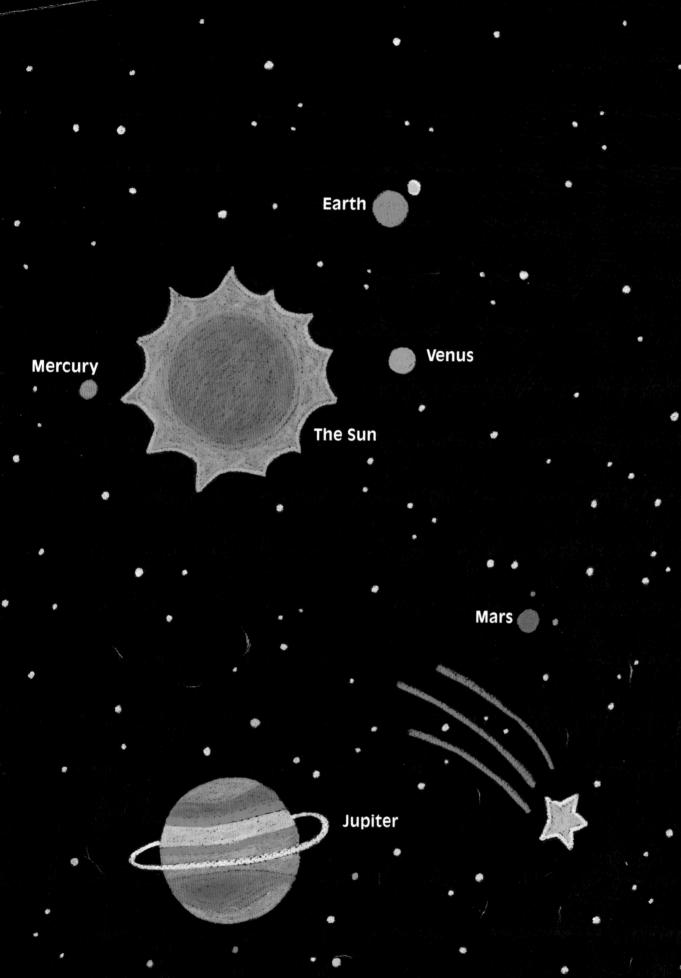

Earth

Venus

Mercury

The Sun

Mars

Jupiter

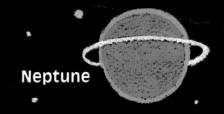

Neptune

Saturn

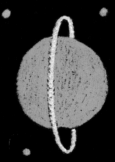

Uranus

Pluto